Jak's Story

Jak's Story

text and illustrations by Aaron Bell

DUNDURN PRESS
TORONTO

Editor: Michael Carroll
Design: Courtney Horner
Printer: Webcom

Library and Archives Canada Cataloguing in Publication

Bell, Aaron, 1971-
        Jak's story / Aaron Bell

ISBN 978-1-55488-710-1

        I. Title.

PS8603.E5IJ36 2010   jC813'.6   C2009-907460-5

1   2   3   4   5   14   13   12   11   10

  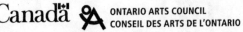

Conseil des Arts   Canada Council
du Canada   for the Arts

Canadä

ONTARIO ARTS COUNCIL
CONSEIL DES ARTS DE L'ONTARIO

We acknowledge the support of the **Canada Council for the Arts** and the **Ontario Arts Council** for our publishing program. We also acknowledge the financial support of the **Government of Canada** through the **Canada Book Fund** and **The Association for the Export of Canadian Books**, and the **Government of Ontario** through the **Ontario Book Publishers Tax Credit program**, and the **Ontario Media Development Corporation**.

Care has been taken to trace the ownership of copyright materials used in this book. The author and the publisher welcome any information enabling them to rectify any references or credits in subsequent editions.

J. Kirk Howard, President

Published by Dundurn Press
Printed and bound in Canada.
www.dundurn.com

Dundurn Press
3 Church Street, Suite 500
Toronto, Ontario, Canada
M5E 1M2

Gazelle Book Services Limited
White Cross Mills
High Town, Lancaster, England
LA1 4XS

Dundurn Press
2250 Military Road
Tonawanda, NY
U.S.A. 14150

As this is my first book (of hopefully many more!),
I would like to dedicate *Jak's Story* to my father,
who passed away suddenly last year.
See, Dad, I can do things on my own ...

Acknowledgements

All living things have a spirit. It is your choice to recognize ...

First, I would like to acknowledge all First Nations people for their gifts to this land. The words of the stories in this book are not traditional, but the teachings woven within the words are immortal. It doesn't matter what the colour of your skin is, for all children are born the same colour without prejudice. These teachings are for them.

I would also like to thank my loving wife, Barb. And also my little ones: Joey, Chelsey, Daxxon, Kierra, and, of course, Jak. This book is for them because, long after I am gone, my words will still be here for their children and grandchildren.

Lastly, I would like to thank my mother and Barb's parents: Gail (Grandma) Bell, Carol (Nana) Nicholson, and Malcolm (Papa) Nicholson. We love you all!

As I am still on the learning path, I often make mistakes. All mistakes are my own and not the publisher's. For those who are offended, I apologize and look forward to any communication in this regard.

Chi miigwetch and many *nya:wehs*. Thank you!

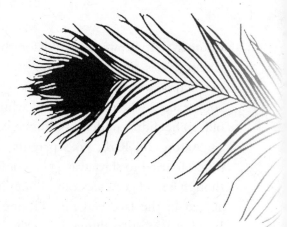

Chapter One

Jak Loren ran as fast as he could. He had dropped his lunch bag along the side of the road but would deal with his parents about that later. His heart was thumping hard and he was losing his breath, but he had to make it home before Steve Burke caught up with him.

Brantford, where Jak lived, was a small city in southwestern Ontario. His parents were fond of saying that his hometown was the only place that hadn't recovered from the Great Depression in the 1930s. Jak didn't know about that, but he did know that Brantford was a pretty good town with good people and that his school, Woodman Drive Public, was great, too. Trees lined most streets in Brantford, including his own, and in the fall everyone gathered their leaves in pumpkin-coloured garbage bags and left them by the side of the road like Halloween jack-o'-lanterns. In spring, like it was now, the big maples in the city were in full leaf.

Jak lived in a small house near Mohawk Park. When he was younger, he splashed around in the park's public wading pool in summer, but he was too old for that now at twelve. Jak's sister, Chelsey, was fifteen going on twenty-five and didn't spend too much time worrying about him. His younger brother, Joey, was cool, except when he cried and whined. Joey was only six months old, so he didn't understand much yet.

Aaron and Barb, Jak's parents, argued a lot and that worried him. He tried to stay away from confrontations when he was home, though he did get a kick out of bugging his sister. Just seeing her get all red in the face was fun. Playing video games and surfing the Internet were two things Jak really liked doing, too. But when his parents started bickering, he went exploring in the nearby ravine. Jak was a gamer, but not the type who spent hours and hours in front of a screen. He had a few computer pals and spoke with them online through his nifty built-in camera and microphone. Often Jak felt that his only friends were the ones he had on the Net.

Now, thinking about the ravine, Jak had a brainstorm. He always felt he could run faster through the woods than on the streets. Jak knew every rock, gully, and tree in the ravine. Glancing over his shoulder, he spotted Steve chugging along with grim determination. He figured he had enough time to take the shortcut between his street and Glenwood Drive. That gave him more energy, and his feet danced over the pavement as he darted between the houses on either side of where the shortcut began.

"You're a little weasel, Jak Loren, and I'm going to catch you eventually!" yelled Steve.

Jak could tell from the tone in Steve's voice that the bully was going to give up soon, so he sprinted even faster. Steve hadn't always gone to Jak's school. In fact, the guy had come from a school that had had a mysterious fire, forcing all the students to go to different schools. Half ended up at Woodman Drive and the other half went somewhere else. When Jak first met Steve, the boy didn't have any lunch, so Jak offered to share his. Steve then hung around Jak all the time, which made Jak uncomfortable. So he told Steve he needed to be by himself once in a while, and Steve got really angry. Ever since that day Steve had Jak in his sights and picked on him constantly.

Steve was a little husky for his age. The guy was smart and all that, probably smarter then Jak, but he never showed it. When Steve put his head down and glared at you, his neck disappeared into his body, making him look like a battle troll in one of the *Lord of the Rings* movies. Steve's voice was husky, just like his body. His whisper could be heard across the classroom, which usually got him into trouble. Steve's smile had two sides: the happy one and the hunter's. When Steve had the hunter's grin, look out! That meant he was about to pounce on his prey. And lately Steve's prey was always Jak.

The ravine was coming up, so Jak increased his speed as he hurtled down into the bushes, dodging to the left and bounding over the rocks in a stream. He jumped and pivoted from rock to rock until he came to the path that his own feet had worn through the woods over the past summers. Behind him Steve was crashing into the ravine, attempting to follow. When Jak heard a splash, he smiled, knowing Steve had fallen into the water.

"You ... you little creep!" Steve sputtered. "Just wait till tomorrow! I'll get you at school!"

Jak didn't take the time to look back. He had to concentrate on where his feet were going and what his head might hit as he dashed through the woods. Jak got into the rhythm of dodging this branch, ducking that one, jumping over that log, while keeping his feet moving. Although he knew tomorrow would be another day of trying to stay out of Steve's clutches, he focused on what had upset Steve so much today.

As he came out of the ravine and into his backyard, he was pretty sure he hadn't done anything in particular to upset the bully. Then Jak thought back to recess when he was playing soccer with the rest of the boys in his class. All the girls were watching and some were playing. He remembered because Christina Lowman was there. Christina was cool, so cool that Jak could never, ever, talk to her. Jak had just gotten the ball, and Steve was trying a little harder than usual to get it away from him. Making a quick deke to his right, Jak then moved left with the ball. Steve tripped, and all the kids giggled, but Christina laughed. She *really* laughed. That was it! Jak now knew why Steve was so angry at him.

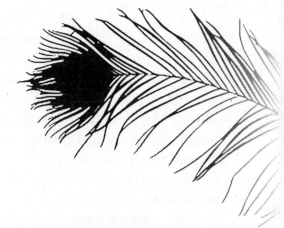

Chapter Two

Jak entered his house through the side door because his parents had decided the front entrance was the "good" one now. Every few years his parents changed which door the family used on a regular basis. Guests and relatives were allowed to use the "good" door, but the rest of the family had to come through the side. It was kind of like switching the towels in the bathroom when guests visited. Jak couldn't understand why his parents had to appear so much better than they actually were. He felt his parents should know who they were and not care what everyone else thought.

As soon as he took off his shoes, Jak heard his parents fighting again, with Joey crying in the background. Jak wanted to go to his brother but knew that would likely land him in the middle of his parents' argument. His parents would never physically hurt Joey, but Jak figured their loud voices scared the baby a whole lot.

Usually, Jak kept to himself. PlayStation 3 and his computer were always there for him. He wasn't very big or tall, but his respectful manner earned praise from adults. With kids his own age, however, he was always being teased. He was quiet in school and that wasn't cool. Jak had heard his parents say he was a loner. He could play almost every sport but didn't like to take part in the teasing and yelling that often happened. Jak really loved soccer, though, since he could usually outrun and outmanoeuvre other players without a problem.

Silently, Jak made his way down to the family room in the basement where his sister was sitting on the couch and reading a celebrity gossip magazine. "They're at it again, huh?"

"Sure are," Chelsey said, one eye glued to the magazine and the other trained on the television. "We get mail every day and in the mail are bills."

Jak plopped himself into a chair and listened to the heated voices upstairs. "They've been fighting a lot lately."

Chelsey grunted. "Get used to it."

Jak knew the fighting bothered Chelsey, but she would never admit it. Chelsey had changed a lot lately and seemed like a stranger to him. He scooped up the TV remote from the coffee table and flipped the channel.

Chelsey looked up from the magazine and scowled. "What are you doing? I was watching that!"

"You're reading."

"So? I can do both, can't I?"

"What was happening on the TV just now?"

"Who cares? I was still watching it!"

"C'mon, Chels, you weren't watching."

She jumped out of her chair, charged at Jak, and yanked the remote from his hand. "I was, too!"

Jak stuck his tongue out.

"Mom, Jak's making faces at me again!"

"I was not, Mom!"

"Were, too!"

Footsteps thundered down the stairs. "What's going on here?" their father demanded. "You both just got home and you're already fighting."

"He took the remote when I was watching my show!" Chelsey whined.

"She wasn't watching!" Jak insisted. "She was reading that stupid magazine!"

"I read this because I like to know about people on TV!" She threw the magazine at Jak's head, barely missing.

"Hey!" Jak squawked.

"That's enough!" their father shouted. "We have enough problems without you two arguing about what's on TV or who's reading what. Chelsey was here first and she was being quiet, so she gets to watch TV. Jak, go to your room and find something to do."

Jak shot a sour look at his sister and stood. "Not fair!"

His father's gaze hardened. "Jak, you can go to your room and find something to do or go outside, but you're not staying down *here* and starting another fight with your sister."

"Fine, I'll go outside."

"Fine," his father said grimly.

"Fine," Jak parroted.

"Enough, Jak! Just go outside, cool down, and come back in for dinner."

"Fine." Jak put on his shoes and shuffled out into the sunlight, happy to get away from his sister and parents.

Chapter Three

Jak picked his way into the ravine, hopping over a fallen tree and ploughing through the thick brush. Why didn't his father believe he hadn't started the fight with Chelsey? It was all her fault. She was always trying to seem grown up and treated him as if he were a baby, which he hated. Chelsey was only three years older than he was. Big deal! Jak kicked at a stick on the path. Remembering he had a granola bar in his jacket pocket, he took it out, ripped off the wrapper, and dropped the paper on the path. A chipmunk chattered at him from a nearby tree.

"What do you want, you stupid thing?" Jak muttered as he picked up the wrapper sheepishly and stuck it in his pocket. He took a bite, then glanced at the chipmunk. "I guess you want some." Sighing, he broke off a piece of the bar and tossed it to the chipmunk. The little animal ignored the granola chunks and continued to chatter at him. Jak shrugged. "Suit yourself."

As he trudged through the woods, he heard what sounded like

voices. Jak didn't want to deal with anybody right now, especially if the voices belonged to adults, who never understand anything important. Sunlight filtered through the leafy maples and oaks, making everything sparkle.

There was a special place Jak considered his own in the ravine, so he headed in that direction. When he arrived in a small clearing surrounded by trees and bushes, the great granite rock was there as it always was. Jak sat beside the rock and looked up at the sky. The whisper of the wind through the ravine made him feel a little better.

He thought about his parents and his sister and brother. Aaron wasn't his real dad. Jak's mother had left him long ago and didn't say much about him. Jak liked Aaron and considered him his father, even though Aaron always told him that no one can replace a person's real dad. Right from the beginning Aaron had said that Jak and Chelsey could call him "Dad" or "Aaron." Either one was fine with him. Jak appreciated that but didn't know why. Maybe he would figure that out later when he was older.

Aaron had two other children from a former marriage. Their names were Kierra and Daxxon, and they visited sometimes but not much. Aaron was an artist and worked at home. He had a small room in their house where he kept all his artist's tools, including pencils, pastels, charcoals, watercolours, and paper and canvas boards of all sizes.

Jak's mom had just started back to work and wasn't happy leaving Joey, but they needed the money. She didn't mind her job at a distribution centre for grocery stores, but felt she could do better. And she missed being with Joey. That made Jak a little jealous of his baby brother, especially since he got so much attention from their mother. But he still thought it was neat having a brother, even if they were pretty far apart in age.

Suddenly, Jak thought again about the bickering his parents were doing lately, and all the fights he seemed to be having with Chelsey. He wished he could make his family just like the ones on TV. They were happy most of the time. Jak was particularly sad about the way things were with his sister. They used to be a team and stuck up for each other. Now all they did was squabble. Why couldn't everything be the way it was before? Why did things have to change? Jak took a deep breath and let it out in a long *whoosh*.

"If you share your food with me, I will tell you a story," whispered a voice beside his ear.

Jak jumped up, dropped his granola bar, and searched around him. Was there someone else here?

Chapter Four

"Who's there?" Jak cried, spinning in a circle. He was sure he had heard a voice, but he didn't understand the language. Jak looked up, too, just in case, but there was still no one in the woods with him. He glanced down and saw that his granola bar was at the base of the Great Rock. Jak bent to pick it up, and the voice spoke again.

"I said, if you share your food with me, I will share a story with you."

Jak froze. It sounded as if the voice was coming from the Great Rock itself! The voice was soft and seemed to flow with the wind. Jak wasn't afraid, since the tone of the voice didn't seem threatening. He peered closer at the Great Rock and saw the moss growing along its rough surface. Jak reached out to touch the stone but decided against it.

"I'm sorry," Jak said, not budging, his eyes gliding slowly over the rock. "What did you say?"

"If you share your catch with me, I will share a story with you," whispered the voice.

Jak was positive the voice was coming from the Great Rock but couldn't understand what was being said. It was a different language. But that was impossible! Rocks couldn't talk. Jak stood straight and looked around once more. Someone had to be doing this, but he couldn't see anyone, so he decided to take a chance.

"I can't understand you," he said, his eyes the only things moving.

The voice sighed, then said, "If you share your food with me, I will share a story with you."

This time Jak was certain. The voice was definitely coming from the Great Rock. Jak could understand the voice now, since it was speaking English.

He took a few steps back to see where the speakers were. Obviously, someone was playing a joke on him. Maybe it was Steve! Jak spun around with wide eyes. He couldn't spot anything, so he walked around the Great Rock to check things there. He couldn't see any wires or speakers anywhere, so he decided to take another chance. "What kind of story? Did you want my granola bar?"

"A very old story, and yes, I have never seen one of those before," the Great Rock said. "It smells good, though."

Jak laughed. "You have a nose? Where is it?"

"*Harumph,*" the Great Rock snorted. "Not everything is as you see it."

Jak glanced all around him again, fearful someone might be watching him speak with a rock. Wouldn't that be something for Steve Burke to find out? Jak would never hear the end of it! Still, he was curious. What kind of story could a rock tell?

"All right," Jak finally said. "You can have my granola bar."

"*Miigwetch,* thank you. I saw you running from another boy. Why was he chasing you?"

Jak studied his feet. "Oh, that was just Steve Burke. He's a kid who picks on me all the time."

"I see. Then sit and listen to Grandfather Rock."

This was the craziest thing Jak had ever experienced, but he sat and listened, anyway.

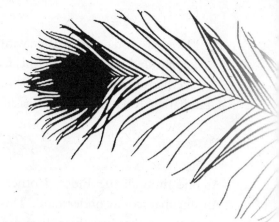

Chapter Five

"At one time all of the Anishinabae —" Grandfather Rock began.

"What's *Anish-nii-bee* mean?" Jak interrupted.

"Little one, you will never learn anything if you do not have the patience to listen."

"Yeah, but what's it mean?"

Grandfather Rock was silent for a long time, then said, "I will answer that question and that question only. After I have answered, you must wait until the end of the story if you have any more questions."

Jak felt as if he were in school and was in trouble for not listening to a teacher. He sensed he had disappointed Grandfather Rock and that made him feel guilty. "All right," he said at last.

"You know the People as Ojibway, but the Ojibway call themselves Anishinabae. In English that means 'The Straight People' or 'The Honest People.' They are one of the oldest peoples of this land."

"Oh ..."

"Now, are you ready to listen with open ears and a closed mouth?"
Jak nodded and glanced at his feet sheepishly.

"Perhaps if you just listen, all your questions will be answered."
Grandfather Rock then began his story.

At one time all the Elder Brother Animals could speak, and the
Anishinabae could understand. This land is very old and there are
many things that have been forgotten, but that is another story.

Now Bear was the largest of his kind, and long ago bears walked
on two legs. Bear did not just walk, though. He threw his chest out
and stuck his nose high in the air because he was the biggest, most
handsome bear of all. He also had a beautiful tail that had all the
colours of the fall leaves within it. As Bear walked with his chest out
and his nose up, he swished his tail back and forth to show everyone
how beautiful it was.

This story, I should mention, took place when the snow was
upon Mother Earth. Everything was white. One day Bear was
strolling through the woods when he came to the edge of a frozen
lake. Out upon this lake sat Fox. Fox had dug a hole in the ice and
was sitting with his back to the hole, looking over his shoulder.

Bear was very confused. When Bear got confused, he flicked his
tail back and forth every which way. *What was Fox doing sitting on
the ice?* Bear thought. *His butt must be getting very cold.*

At that moment Fox jumped into the air. Biting his tail was a
fish! Fox was using his tail to fish through the hole in the ice. Bear
was stunned. Fox had just caught a fish with his tail! Bear thought
to himself, *Fox could only catch a tiny fish because he only had a little
tail.* Bear had an idea. If Fox taught Bear how to catch a fish with
Bear's tail, Bear could catch the biggest fish in the lake. So Bear
thrust his chest out, stuck his nose in the air, and approached Fox.

When Bear was close to Fox, he said, "Fox, I want you to teach
me how to catch a fish with my tail."

Fox had seen Bear coming. He was annoyed with Bear because
the larger animal thought he was so much better than all other

creatures. So Fox decided to teach Bear a lesson. Fox twitched his ears, then cocked his head this way and that. Finally, he said, "All right, Bear, I can teach you. But you must listen carefully to everything I say at all times."

"I have magnificent ears!" Bear cried. "Better than any other animal! I will hear you just fine!"

"*Shh!* You must be very quiet. If you make too much noise, the fish will hear and swim away."

"Why, I can be very ..." Bear started to bellow. When he realized he was yelling, though, Bear lowered his voice. "I can be very quiet when I need to be."

"When I tell you to lift your tail," Fox said, "you must move as fast as you can before the fish can let go."

"I have the fastest butt of all animals!" Bear declared.

"All right, Bear, turn around, put your tail in the ice, and wait for my command."

Bear did as Fox told him and sat on the ice with his tail in the cold water. Just then it started to snow — big, fat snowflakes that covered everything. Soon Bear was coated with snow. The snow was so thick that it acted like a heavy blanket over Bear's fur. Bear was very warm now, and he closed his eyes and fell fast asleep.

Fox saw what had happened and giggled. He padded back to his den, turned three times, put his tail over his eyes, and was soon sleeping himself.

The next day Fox woke and came out of his den. He stretched and yawned and gave greetings to Father Sun. When he looked out over the frozen lake, he spied a large white lump. Fox realized that Bear had spent the entire night on the ice! That gave Fox an idea. He padded out quietly to Bear, put his muzzle against Bear's ear, took a deep breath, and yelled at the top of his lungs, "Now, Bear, lift your tail!"

Bear spun around, throwing snow everywhere. He searched for his magnificent fish, but all he saw was Fox running away as fast as possible. Bear was bewildered, and when he was like that, he swished his gorgeous tail back and forth. However, as Bear tried to move his tail, he realized it was gone! He glanced down and saw that his tail was stuck in the ice.

To this day bears always travel on four legs to hide their stubby little tails. Bear will never forget how tiny Fox tricked him into tearing his own tail right off.

When Jak realized Grandfather Rock was finished his story, he laughed so hard that the birds in the trees peered down and ruffled their feathers.

"Also know," Grandfather Rock continued, "that when Bear walks he shakes his head back and forth, grunting his annoyance at Fox the whole time. The times we see Bear on two legs now is when he is looking for sneaky Fox."

Jak shut his eyes and imagined himself as Fox, with Steve Burke as Bear. Nodding to himself, Jak decided he would never act like Bear. Steve might try to beat him up, but Steve would never catch Jak with his chest out, thinking he was better than anyone else.

"Thanks for the story," Jak whispered. The woods were now silent, and Jak felt the need to whisper. He looked up through the leaves in the trees and realized it was getting late. The clouds had turned that dusty pink when the sun was about to sink below the horizon. "I have to go home now."

"If you bring another gift tomorrow, I can share another story with you," Grandfather Rock said as Jak left the clearing.

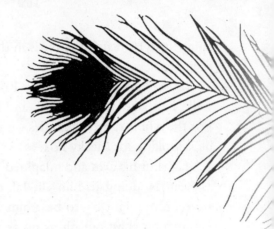

Chapter Six

"Where were you?" Jak's father demanded when he came in the door.

Jak thought that was a silly question. After all, Aaron had told him to go outside or to his room. Jak knew his father wouldn't appreciate him answering that way. Nor would it be a good idea to tell Aaron about Grandfather Rock or the story the voice had told him. Who would ever believe that? Jak wasn't even certain he believed it himself. "I was out exploring the ravine," he finally told his father.

Chelsey snorted. "Jak's always climbing trees and chasing squirrels. Maybe he should just live out there."

Jak glared at his sister. Sometimes she was cool, but just now wasn't one of those occasions. Actually, it had been a long time since she had been cool.

"Leave him alone, Chelsey!" Jak's father ordered. "Stop bickering, both of you, and sit down for supper."

At the dining-room table Joey squealed in his high chair. Jak's mother turned to Chelsey and asked how her day had been. She mumbled something in the monotone voice she always used these days. Jak could tell that Chelsey's attitude upset his mother, but as usual Barb didn't say anything. The ways of adults were strange to Jak. He hoped that when he was an adult he would remember times like this and act differently.

Jak picked at his food and ate slowly the way he usually did. His father was already finished and off to do more work in the basement on the computer. Aaron worked at home, but a few times each month he was gone for many days at a time. Even when his father was home, Jak felt he didn't really see much of him, and that bothered him.

Joey bit on his spoon as Jak's mother tried to feed him squished-up carrots. *Babies sure ate disgusting things!* Jak thought.

Just then Aaron rushed back upstairs. "Hey, did you know they're building new homes across the way?"

Jak's mother turned from feeding Joey. "Across the ravine?"

"Yep!" Jak's father replied. "Maybe some new kids will move into the area for you to make friends with, Jak."

Across the ravine? Jak thought. *Where across the ravine? There was nothing except trees there.*

"There's a community meeting tonight in the school gym about this," Aaron said. "I think we should find out what's happening." He looked at his wife.

Jak's mother nodded as she smiled at Joey, while Chelsey sighed as if to say, "Whatever."

Jak wasn't certain what he wanted to do. Then he had a terrible thought, and his heart nearly leaped into his throat. They were going to cut down his trees! They were going to put more stupid houses in his private playground! And what about Grandfather Rock? What would happen to him?

Aaron must have noticed Jak's frantic expression. "What's wrong?" he asked.

Jak glanced at his feet and mumbled, "Nothing. Can I be excused?"

Barb looked at Aaron, then at Jak, and said, "I guess so. You aren't hungry? You hardly touched your supper."

"I'm actually kind of full," Jak said.

"Go ahead then."

Jak rose from the table, tousled Joey's hair as he passed, and headed to his room glumly. What was he going to do? He couldn't let them cut down the trees. Didn't they know the trees had been there a lot longer and had a right to be there? He didn't want to talk to his parents about this. He also didn't want to speak to Chelsey about it, either. She was in one of her moods and would probably throw something at him. Then it hit Jak. He could let Grandfather Rock know about all of this after school tomorrow night. Maybe Grandfather Rock would know what to do to stop the construction.

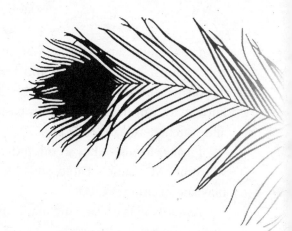

Chapter Seven

The gymnasium at Woodman Drive Public School wasn't very big. Chairs were set up facing the stage at one end of the gym. On the stage were a table and a large map of Jak's neighbourhood behind it. Sitting at the table were people Jak had never seen before. At one end there was a woman with her hair in a bun on top of her head. Jak thought she might be a librarian from the look of her. At the other end of the table was a mousy little man who constantly picked up papers and organized them. He wore a tie that made his head look larger than his body. That probably wasn't true, but Jak grinned at the thought of the store where the man had bought the tie.

Sitting between the librarian and Mousy Man was someone Jak instantly didn't like. The man sported shiny sunglasses even indoors. He was pretty muscular and wore a bright yellow construction hat. Because of the sunglasses, Jak couldn't see where the man was looking, so it seemed as if he were always staring directly at Jak, which was creepy.

Jak's family sat in the middle of the chairs on the gym floor. Joey whined a little but was too busy gazing at everything to be concerned about much else. Chelsey had a "I'm so bored and don't know why I'm here" expression pasted on her face. Jak simply sat and watched as people filed in.

Finally, Mousy Man stood and cleared his throat. "Hello and welcome. My name's Pablo Shriken, and I'm the developer of this new and exciting project."

As soon as Jak heard the man's name, he forgot it. Mousy Man suited him better, anyway.

Mousy Man droned on for a while about what the project was all about, how many houses were going to be built, how great a boon to the community it would be, and so on and so on. Then he smiled toothily and said, "Now I'd like to introduce Mr. Stone, our project manager. He'll explain the process we're going to take." Mousy Man motioned to the man in sunglasses.

Mr. Stone seemed to inflate and become even bigger. He didn't take off his sunglasses or the yellow construction hat. "Good evening, ladies and gentlemen. I'd like to thank all of you for coming."

Jak knew that what was coming next wasn't going to be good. When adults thanked you for being somewhere, it was because they wanted something.

"I'm going to quickly explain what will happen over the next few months," Mr. Stone said in his gravelly voice. It was almost as if he had to crush pebbles with his throat to be heard. "Once we have the signatures necessary to begin construction, we'll clear all the terrain marked in red on the map behind me." Mr. Stone gestured over his shoulder. "Our company is well regarded within this community as being fast and efficient. Let's face it, we all know that loud construction equipment can be annoying. Considering we work beside it all the time, we completely understand why some people would be irritated at all the noise."

There were a few grunts of agreement from the audience.

Mr. Stone continued. "We promise that all the heavy equipment will finish work in as short a time as possible. We estimate that it will take us less than a month to clear the terrain and create the

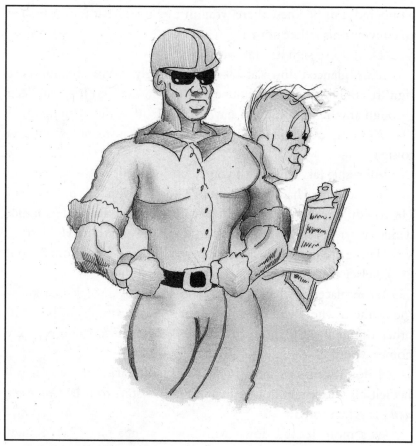

foundations for the new homes."

Jak peered at the map. Suddenly, he realized that the area marked in red indicated most of the ravine in his backyard and beyond. Jak's chest hurt. Less than a month to clear all the trees and bushes that had been his only friends for the past few summers? That didn't seem fair at all.

"Mr. Shriken will now pass out forms for your signatures," Mr. Stone said. "Basically, the signatures will let us know you've been informed of the construction and that you're aware there will be some noise over the next little while. Once we have all the signatures necessary, we can begin with this new endeavour to better our community and invite more people to live with us here."

Jak got up with his parents and moved toward the table that held the signature forms. Where was the form for kids to sign? Jak wondered, but he knew there wouldn't be one. That meant he had to convince his father not to sign.

"Dad, don't sign it," Jak whispered.

Aaron glanced down at Jak questioningly. "Why shouldn't we sign? It's only going to be about a month of noise, and Joey can sleep through anything. You don't have to be afraid of the equipment."

"I'm not scared of the equipment, Dad. I just don't want you to sign."

"All right, Jak, why don't you?" Aaron asked.

Jak realized he hadn't thought of a good reason. His mind raced. He couldn't really tell Aaron about Grandfather Rock. His father would never believe him. He had to think of something else fast!

"Those are my trees," Jak whispered, looking away from Aaron.

Chelsey laughed, and her parents glared at her.

Aaron placed his hands on his son's shoulders. "Jak … I know the ravine is where you play. But sometimes, for things to be built, other things have to be torn down. Besides, once there are new homes, you'll have some new friends, right?"

"I don't want any new friends. I like the ravine the way it is." Jak felt his cheeks get hot again and his eyes start to tear. *Oh, please don't cry!* he thought.

Jak's mom leaned down with Joey on her hip. "Jak, honey, it will be better for the community. It means new jobs and new money coming in. Who knows? There could even be a playground built for Joey."

Jak knew then that he wouldn't be able to convince his parents not to sign, and his chest hurt a whole lot more as the first tears trickled down his cheeks. Mr. Stone walked by at that moment and seemed to stare at Jak for a split second. All Jak could do was shiver.

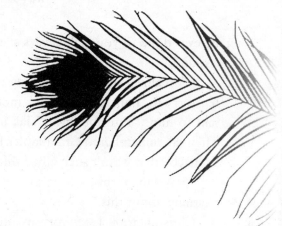

Chapter Eight

Steve Burke cornered Jak the next day at school. "Where are you going to run now, you little snot!" he yelled during recess.

Jak stood his ground and glanced around him. A circle of kids had gathered, sensing something was going to happen. "I'm not running this time."

All the kids gasped. No one had ever talked back to Steve Burke before. They all moved a little closer. Steve seemed stunned for a moment, then his eyes darkened, his shoulders hunched, and he lurched forward.

"Steve Burke, you big bully, leave him alone!" someone cried shrilly. "What's he ever done to you?"

Jak and Steve turned and saw Christina Lowman with her hands on her hips. She was glaring at Steve. Jak's heart skipped a beat. Christina was the most popular and prettiest girl in his class. And she was sticking up for him!

"Can't you see Jak's smaller than you?" Christina asked. "What's he ever done to you? Jak always stays by himself and doesn't make a sound."

Jak realized she wasn't sticking up for him, after all. Instead she felt sorry for him. That hurt Jak more than anything Steve had ever said to him. "I'm not small," Jak insisted, but no one heard him. Then Jak remembered Grandfather Rock's Fox story. Fox was small, so maybe that wasn't such a bad thing.

"Stay out of this, Christina," Steve growled. "You don't know anything about this."

Christina took a step forward and looked Steve in the eye. "Are you saying I'm stupid?"

Steve seemed confused and dismayed.

Jak knew Steve was fond of Christina. Who wasn't?

"No, I'm … I'm not saying you're —" Steve sputtered.

"I think you just did, Steven Burke. I'm going to tell the teacher." Christina turned and stomped off with the determination that only a twelve-year-old girl can muster. She was followed by a flock of her friends, all peering over their shoulders with anger in their eyes.

Steve knew he had to make a choice. He could stay and teach Jak a lesson or he could try to apologize to Christina. Jak saw the indecision in Steve's eyes and waited for him to decide. He recalled the story Grandfather Rock had shared with him and tried not to think he was better than Steve.

Finally, Steve turned and chased after Christina. "Wait, wait, Christina! I'm not going to do anything! Wait!"

Jak was left alone in the middle of the field as the gang of kids melted away when they realized nothing was going to happen. They knew, just as Jak did, that this wasn't over. Jak would have to tread carefully during the next few days. He was still thinking about how he could stay out of Steve's way when the bell rang, ending recess.

Chapter Nine

Jak sat at his desk and gazed at the chalkboard decorated with the alphabet and sayings from famous people. He brought out his history textbook and workbook and waited for the teacher to begin. Jak saw Scott White and the weird new kid pass a note to each other. The weird kid giggled, and Scott winked and looked around as if he were the greatest spy ever. Jak then felt a poke at his back and twisted to see Shelley Turner.

"What did you ever do to Steve Burke to make him so mad at you?" she whispered.

Jak glanced at Steve, who was glowering at him. "I didn't really do anything. All I did was play soccer with him, and he didn't like the way I was playing."

The reality was that Jak was a much better soccer player than Steve was, and that made Steve jealous. He wasn't going to tell Shelley Turner that, though. As soon as he did, it would be all over the school during lunch hour. Shelley was the type of girl who was a friend one day and then hated you the next. Plus, she couldn't keep a secret at all.

"All right, everyone, we're going to start our First Nations unit now, so please take out your workbooks and write what I'm putting on the board," Mr. Crick, the teacher, said.

Jak didn't mind Mr. Crick much. He had a bad last name but that wasn't his fault. Jak smiled as he recalled how the class got on Mr. Crick's nerves by chirping like crickets. Then he looked up at the board and began to write: "Iroquois, Six Nations." Jak liked learning about the First Nations people. "Lived in longhouses that ranged in length from fifteen metres to one hundred and fifty metres. These were the very first apartment buildings. In some longhouses two hundred and fifty people lived together."

Sometimes Jak wished he lived back when the woods ruled the land. He imagined a place like that and smiled. Still, he would have missed his PlayStation 3. "The original Five Nations of the Iroquoian Confederacy are: Mohawk, Seneca, Cayuga, Oneida, and Onondaga. In the early 1700s the Tuscarora joined the original Five Nations to make them Six."

The other kids in the class started to get antsy with all the writing they were doing. Usually, Mr. Crick gave handouts for everyone to add to their binders. This seemed to take a lot longer. Jak heard various whispers as the scratching of pencils on paper overlapped the sound of the chalk on the board.

"Holy cow! Is he writing a book?"

"Why can't we just dictate this into one of those voice-analyzer things on the computer?"

"My hand already hurts! Geez!"

"Mr. Crick, why can't you just give us a handout?" the new weird kid asked.

Mr. Crick turned from the board. "It's important for you to understand that the First Nations people were here before us, and I know that if I give you a handout, you'll just put it away and not read it until you have to. If I write on the board and you have to copy it, you have to read it now."

There was a collective sigh around the room.

"Did you know that the First Nations taught without pencils?" Mr. Crick asked them. "They taught through the spoken word. Children were taught to listen first. Stories were passed down for thousands of years. That was, and still is, the way First Nations teach."

Jak's eyebrows rose. Grandfather Rock had said the exact same thing ... sort of.

"You talk all the time," the weird kid said, and the class giggled.

Mr. Crick frowned. "Yes, but do you actually listen?"

The students looked everywhere but at Mr. Crick, who continued to write on the board: "Matrilineal society. Longhouses are run by the clan mothers. Clan mothers choose the chiefs. Woman are the decision-makers and men are the speakers."

The whispers started again.

"My hand really hurts now."

"I wish I had my computer here. I can type a lot faster than I can write."

"This is a book. He's making us copy a book!"

"This isn't *the* book," Jak muttered. "It's just the introduction."

The class erupted in laughter, and Jak glanced up. Everyone in the class, including Steve and Christina, was laughing. But they weren't making fun of him. They were laughing at what he had said. He hadn't realized he had spoken so loudly. Then the laughter increased as Mr. Crick looked directly at him.

"Mr. Loren," Mr. Crick said, "I think you should concentrate on the words on the board and not share your personal thoughts with the class."

Jak stared at his workbook, and the laughter stopped, but there were still snickers throughout the class. *Maybe I should always share what I'm thinking,* Jak thought. *Maybe I'm kind of funny.*

When Jak looked up again, he saw Christina studying him with bright eyes. Jak immediately shifted his gaze to his paper and continued to write. He liked it when Christina noticed him but never knew what to do when she did. When he peeked at her again, she was whispering to her friends. That made Jak nervous. What was she whispering about? Then he noticed Steve Burke staring at him.

Jak didn't break eye contact with Steve. He remembered what Grandfather Rock had shared with him. He didn't want to be better than anyone. He wanted to be Fox. Jak met Steve's eyes without any malice. He merely returned the other boy's gaze, confident within himself. A slight smile crossed Steve's face. Not a smile of anger, but a smile of respect. That really confused Jak.

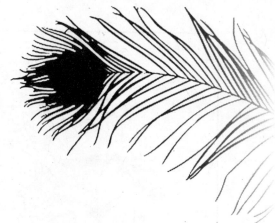

Chapter Ten

That day, after school, Jak ran all the way home and grabbed an apple. He told his parents he was going into the ravine and practically flew out the door and into the backyard before they could say anything. Then he launched himself into the ravine and scrambled down its slope until he was at the bottom.

When the birds spotted Jak, they stopped singing, but as soon as they realized he wasn't going to hurt them, they started up again. Jak raced through the woods with the music of singing birds in his ears and a smile on his face.

His good mood was shattered, though, when he heard the sound of an engine close by. Jak halted and looked around. The birds had also ceased singing, and the ravine seemed unnaturally quiet. The engine roared louder and appeared to be coming from the other side of the woods. Carefully, Jak made his way through the prickly bushes until he spotted a great yellow machine being off-loaded from an even larger truck. Men in yellow and orange

hats with shiny reflective vests waved and yelled to one another.

Finally, the big yellow machine was on the ground. Thick black smoke rose from its exhaust and filled the air with an awful smell. When the machine was finally turned off, Jak heard two men speaking with each other.

"Tomorrow or the next day is when we'll begin clearing this area," one man said.

"We still have to wait for all the community signatures before we can start, right?" the other man asked.

"I don't think there'll be any problems. Most of the homes around here are on the other side of this ravine. This area is all flat and being used for nothing."

"I guess we'll find out soon enough," the second man said.

Jak noticed a car pull up, and out of it came Mr. Stone and

Mousy Man, otherwise known as Mr. Shriken. Apparently, the other two men hadn't noticed them arrive, because when Mr. Stone spoke, they both jumped.

"What's going on?"Mr. Stone demanded. "Why is everyone standing around? We've got work to do here!" He still wore his sunglasses and bright yellow hat.

Jak realized that his ravine was going to be flattened. He gazed into the trees and saw all the birds flicking back and forth. Jak felt sad for the birds whose homes were going to be destroyed. After all, it was early spring and they were making their homes now. Even the raccoons and squirrels that made their houses in the ground and fallen trees would become homeless. Didn't anyone think of them at all?

Slowly, Jak shuffled over to where Grandfather Rock lived. When he came into the clearing, he sat beside Grandfather Rock and put down the apple.

"*Sago,* little one," Grandfather Rock said. "Many *nya:wehs* for this wonderful apple. It has been a long time since I have had an apple."

"You're welcome, Grandfather Rock," Jak said, his eyes clouded with sadness. The birds started to sing again around them, and he could hear squirrels rustling in the trees.

"Is something wrong?" Grandfather Rock asked.

Jak shook his head and kept his eyes downcast. He didn't want to tell Grandfather Rock about the construction that was going on. Not yet, anyway. "No, not really ..." he finally whispered.

"Would you like to hear another story?" Grandfather Rock asked.

Jak glanced up. "Yes, please!"

"Have you ever chased butterflies?"

"Yes, but they're hard to catch without a net."

"What did you do when you caught one?"

Jak thought for a moment. "I kept it for a little while, but then I felt bad and let it go."

"I can tell you why you let it go."

Jak stared at Grandfather Rock. He had already told him why he had let it go. Hadn't Grandfather Rock been listening? Still, Jak was curious. "Yes, I'd like to learn why I let the butterfly go."

"Then sit with open ears, listen with your heart, and you will soon know," Grandfather Rock said. "This land is very old. Long ago only spirits travelled across the land, and the people were very new here. At that time all could speak with one another and everything worked in a proper way. The Anishinabae, or the Ojibway in your language, lived in a village. Gitche Manitou was one of the most powerful spirits in this place. He was also known as the Creator. He was the one who created most of what you see around you now."

"You're saying there was nothing but ghosts here a long time ago?" Jak asked, his eyes wide.

"Little one, listening is a skill that children need to learn. The more you listen, the more your questions will be answered."

"Sorry," Jak murmured.

"Questions are good, but there are proper times for them. Your responsibility, as a little one, is to ask questions, since you are still young. That is how you learn. But listening is a greater skill. You will not learn the answers to any of your questions if you do not listen."

Jak nodded, making a point not to say another word.

"Let me begin the story then," Grandfather Rock said.

The Creator was walking through the woods one day and had a smile on his face and in his heart, for he was happy. He loved to bring gifts to the children of the Anishinabae people because their laughter was one of the merriest sounds ever heard.

What gift can I bring to the children today? the Creator asked himself. As he thought, his feet swished through the leaves on the ground, and that gave him an idea.

The Creator always carried a satchel with him. This satchel was very special. The things the Creator put into it would often become what the Creator wished them to be. The Creator reached down and scooped some leaves into his hands, then placed them inside the satchel. Shaking the satchel, he made his way to the Anishinabae village. All the children saw him coming and asked, "What have you brought for us today? What have you brought for us today?"

Reaching into his satchel, the Creator took out the leaves. He threw them into the air where they danced this way and that as though they had lives of their own. The children laughed and chased the leaves back and forth across a meadow. But soon, as all leaves do, they fell back onto the ground and the children became bored. The Creator knew he would have to do something different to make the leaves special. So he snatched up the leaves, returned them to his satchel, and told the Anishinabae children he would return the next day. Then the Creator went back into the woods and thought to himself, *How can I make these leaves different?*

Just then the birds around the Creator began to sing louder and louder. He gazed into the trees and saw robins, starlings, blue jays, cardinals, and chickadees. Then a smile spread across the Creator's face. All children loved the sound of music! So he would take the songs of the birds and add them to his leaves, then each leaf would have its own song. The Creator reached into the trees, plucked all the songs from the birds, and added them to his satchel.

The next day the Creator returned to the Anishinabae village. When the children saw him coming, they cried, "What have you brought for us today? What have you brought for us today?"

The Creator reached into his satchel and gathered up the leaves. When he threw them into the air, every leaf had its own gift of song! All of the children chased the leaves, listening to their songs. The Creator watched and drank in the laughter of the children as they played across the land, and he was happy.

One child, though, was sitting alone with his head bowed low. The Creator went to this child and asked him, "Why aren't you playing with my gifts?"

The child gazed up into the Creator's eyes. "Creator, I wish to give you thanks for all the gifts you've brought to my people in the past. But I'm sad. Whenever I have a bad dream or a bad day, I listen to the songs of the birds rising with Father Sun first thing in the morning. Their songs tell me I'm going to have a good day. If your leaves now have the songs of the birds, I'll no longer hear them rising with Father Sun in the east."

The Creator realized he might have made a mistake. He looked into the trees and saw that the robins, blue jays, starlings, and chickadees were unhappy, for their gift of song had been stolen. So the Creator collected all of the leaves once more, put them into his satchel, and returned to the forest. Then, without another thought, he reached into the satchel and gave the birds back their songs.

Still, the Creator wanted to bring another gift to the Anishinabae children, so he walked through the woods some more until he spotted many different types of flowers. He saw tall ones, small ones, thin ones, and fat ones. Each flower was a different colour!

The Creator got another idea, and a smile lit his face. He took one petal from each flower — red, purple, pink, and blue ones! There were tall petals, small petals, thin petals, and fat petals, and all were different colours. He put them all into his satchel with the leaves and returned to the Anishinabae village the next day. Once again all the Anishinabae children saw him coming and cried, "What have you brought for us today? What have you brought for us today?"

When the Creator reached into his satchel this time, out flew the very first butterflies! They danced upon the wind as though they had lives of their own. There were tall butterflies, small butterflies, thin butterflies, and fat butterflies, and all were different colours of red, pink, purple, and blue. The children laughed and danced as they tried to catch the very first butterflies ever found in this place.

To this day, children always try to catch butterflies. But when they catch them, they usually let them go, for all children know that at one time these butterflies were merely leaves upon the trees. At one time these butterflies carried the songs of the birds with them. And all children know never to take advantage of the Creator's gifts.

"So, little one, did you learn something when you returned your butterfly to the winds? Just remember that when you wake up with Father Sun rising in the east first thing in the morning and you hear the songs of the birds, you, too, will always have a very good day."

The birds around Jak swooped into the air, and rising from the ravine floor was a butterfly. It floated slowly on seemingly awkward wings. Then more butterflies lifted off. They had come from nowhere! Jak hadn't noticed them there before. As he watched, more and more butterflies filled the air. They flicked this way and that as they danced upon the wind in a rainbow of colours. The butterflies appeared to move in time with the songs of the birds! Jak watched as they flew around his ears and circled the trees. Then, in what seemed an instant, Jak was sitting by himself once more in front of Grandfather Rock.

Jak was amazed and stunned. He remembered catching his first butterfly and feeling bad. He recalled the softness of its wings and how it had seemed happy even though it was in his hands. Jak had let it go and watched it disappear across the land. Now he felt as

45

though he had learned something he had already known and had forgotten. Slowly, Jak began to smile, then he grinned. He had an idea and knew he had to race back to his house.

"Thank you, Grandfather Rock, for sharing your story with me!" After saying that, Jak ran off.

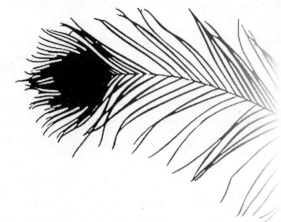

Chapter Eleven

"Dad, Dad, we have to go back to that community meeting about the construction!" Jak cried as he crashed through the door. He stood in the doorway panting, then realized his parents were staring at him strangely. "What's wrong?"

"Nothing's wrong," Jak's mother said. "You got a phone call from someone, though." Both of his parents had silly smiles on their faces.

"Who called?" Jak asked.

The grins on the faces of Jak's parents got bigger. "Christina Lowman called for you," they both said.

Jak's heart leaped. Christina had called him? *Wait a minute!* What could she want? What kind of trick was she playing? And why were his parents grinning at him that way? The expression on Jak's face must have sent a signal to his parents because they both moved out of his way and motioned him to a chair.

"We're going to talk about your girlfriend," Jak's father said.

Jak was terrified! He didn't want to speak to his parents about Christina. *Girlfriend?* He didn't know exactly what she wanted and why. Jak was fairly sure she didn't like him at all. Why would she like him? *Girlfriend?* She had already said he was quiet and small. Jak really wanted to go back to that community meeting and see if he could learn anything new about the construction in the ravine.

"Uh, no thanks. She's not my girlfriend. At least I don't think so, anyway. But that doesn't matter. Can we go back to that community meeting about the construction?"

His parents were confused. Jak could tell. They had both lost their smiles.

"Community meeting?" his father asked. "What are you talking about?"

Jak sighed. "I want to go back to the meeting and tell them why they shouldn't cut down the trees."

"Wait!" Aaron said. "Who's cutting down the trees?"

"The construction workers. They were talking about it while they were taking a big machine off an even bigger truck. That Mr. Stone was there, and so was Mousy Man. I mean, Mr. Shriken."

"You were close to the construction site?"

Jak realized he might have said too much. The looks on his parents' faces weren't good ones. "No, I wasn't near the construction. There wasn't any construction. They were just unloading a big machine. I heard them talking."

"Young man," his father said, "you better not go near any construction … ever! If we catch you near that construction site, you can say goodbye to your PlayStation 3 for a very long time!"

Jak sighed again. "All right, all right, I won't go near the construction site. Now can we go back to the meeting, please?"

His father scratched his head. "We haven't heard anything about another meeting."

Aaron and Barb glanced at each other. They had an expression on their faces that Jak knew all too well. Whenever Joey seemed sick, they had that look. It was a grimace that said, "I don't know what's wrong, but something is."

"Jak, honey, that meeting we went to was the only one," his mother said softly. "We signed the form, remember? There won't be another meeting." She reached for him, but Jak stepped back, desperation making his heart thump.

"Now ... what about this girl?" his father asked.

That smile was back on Aaron's face. Jak couldn't understand why they were so interested in Christina. He didn't want to say anything until he was sure what Christina really wanted. "Nothing's going on! Geez, can I go now?"

"Do you have homework?" his mother asked.

"Nope. I finished it at school."

"Only an hour on that PlayStation tonight, Jak," his father said.

"Okay," Jak replied as he turned to leave. He ruffled Joey's hair as he passed by and was rewarded with a happy gurgle.

Chapter Twelve

The next day at school Christina didn't say a word to Jak. That worried him more then Steve leaving him alone. Jak was surprised but happy that he could relax while in the yard at recess and lunch break. He played soccer with everyone and scored one goal. The teachers were making their rounds in the yard with the regular pack of kids following them. They looked like the swans Jak had seen on television nature shows. The mother swan led her little ones around, and they followed single file. This was a slower version of that. The teachers took a few steps, then the pack of kids followed, repeating the process until the bell rang.

After lunch Jak went to his desk, sat down, and waited for Mr. Crick to begin speaking. On the board there was a drawing of a building. It looked like a big log with holes in the top. Underneath the drawing was the word *longhouse*.

"All right, class," Mr. Crick said, "open your social studies books to page 130 and let's begin."

There was a quiet rustling in the classroom as everyone reached into their desks and moved things around to get their books out.

"Does anyone know what a longhouse was made of?" Mr. Crick asked. "Or what was inside? Or how many people lived in one?"

The students glanced everywhere but at Mr. Crick. It was obvious that most, if not all of them, hadn't read the opening chapter of the textbook. Jak had, however, and raised his hand. Mr. Crick nodded at him.

"The longhouse was made of cedar poles, bass or elm bark, and cordage made from the bark of the cedar tree."

"Yes, that's right, Mr. Loren," Mr. Crick said. "However, that's only a few of the things that went into the construction of a longhouse. The longhouse was basically that — a long house."

A few students giggled.

"The Six Nations people built their homes almost like we build ours today," Mr. Crick continued. "They constructed a frame and then placed layers of basswood bark over the frame. They actually had two layers of bark and between the two layers they put clay and moss for insulation."

A hand went up.

"Yes, Mr. Jackson?"

"Wasn't that a lot of work?" Bill Jackson asked. "Bark isn't very big and they would have had to put a lot of bark onto the frame, right?"

Mr. Crick smiled. "Mr. Jackson, the trees back then were very large because people didn't cut them all down the way they do now. It would take about eight grown men holding hands to reach around an average tree long ago. The people of the Six Nations would actually create a sheet of bark that was very long and tall. They learned to live on this land hundreds of years before Europeans came here."

There was a gasp from the class when Mr. Crick said that.

"And they learned how to shape the wood using water. Plus, they all worked together to build the longhouse. Back then it was hard to keep warm and put a roof over your head. Survival wasn't easy."

Jak could see that his classmates were working that out in their heads. He really couldn't imagine a time when heat and homes were such hard work to come by. Jak figured the Six Nations people had to be very strong.

"The longhouse actually had bunk beds on either side," Mr. Crick said. "The bottom bunk was where the young mothers and newborns slept. The second bunk was where the elders slept, and the third level was where the young warriors slept since they were much more agile and could get down quickly if they needed to. The last bunk was storage space because it was so high. The Six Nations people stored clothes and tools there and hung corn braids from the rafters so they could dry out in the smoke from the firepits."

Christina put up her hand. "What were the floors made of?"

Mr. Crick smiled with satisfaction. He was enjoying this. Jak's class usually didn't ask a lot of questions, which made Mr. Crick unhappy. But he was definitely happy with his class now. "What do you think the floors were made of, Christina?"

Christina had bright blue eyes and curly blond hair down to her shoulders. Some days she wore dresses that made her look beautiful, while other days she wore clothes she could play soccer in. That was why every boy in the class had a crush on her. The only problem was that Christina knew that.

"I think the floors were made of just dirt or grass, right?" Christina said. "Because the Iroquois didn't have carpets and stuff."

Mr. Crick smiled. "You're half right, Christina. The Iroquoian people did live on the land, but they did have carpets. They just weren't the same kind of carpets we have in our homes today. Back then the Iroquois hunted and used everything from the animals they killed. Deer hides were placed on top of corn husk mats to create carpets on the ground. Did you know they actually had freezers back then?"

Steve chirped like a cricket, and the other students giggled. Jak smiled, too, because he knew the class was in a good mood. They were actually learning about something and having fun at the same time. Normally, if Mr. Crick wasn't in a good mood, Steve would have had to stand in the hall for making such a noise. Today Mr. Crick merely smiled.

Jak put up his hand.

"Yes, Mr. Loren?" Mr. Crick said.

"What are elders?"

"Elders are very knowledgeable people within the community. They're the ones who live longer than other people and are considered very smart. The elders are the ones who remember the ceremonies and pass them along to the next generations."

"Sort of like grandparents," the weird kid said.

"Yes, sort of like grandparents," Mr. Crick agreed, "but that isn't how we make a comment in this room, Mr. Smith."

So that was the weird kid's real name, Jak thought.

"We put up our hands if we have a question or comment," Mr. Crick said. "The longhouse was like your home. Except you lived with your *entire* family in the longhouse. Nieces, nephews, aunts, uncles, grandfather, grandmother, Mom, and Dad all lived around the fire. There were other families just like yours, too, living in the longhouse. In fact, you could tell how many families lived in a longhouse by the number of smoke holes in the roof. So you can imagine how many people lived in the longhouse. The longhouse was probably the very first apartment building in North America!"

Jak tried to picture a longhouse with smoke rising from many holes in its roof. He imagined his family living in the longhouse with his aunts and uncles, but he had a hard time visualizing that. Jak couldn't see his sister sitting around a fire. She would be too worried about her hair or her nails or something. He figured he could live there, though. It would be cool.

Chapter Thirteen

Jak made his way through the shortcut on his way home from school. He thought of what Mr. Crick had said about the Six Nations and their longhouses. As he turned into the ravine, he glanced up and saw sunlight lancing through the leaves of the trees. To his left was the fenced backyard of a house with a swimming pool. The trees and bushes went right up to the fence. Obviously, the fences were there to separate the people from the ravine. That made him sad. Jak loved being in the ravine. He could lose himself just in the sound of the wind moving through the trees. In the centre of the ravine ran the stream.

Smiling, Jak walked along the path next to the stream. As he hiked, the noises of the modern world outside the ravine faded away and the sounds of the ravine took over. He heard birds singing and was reminded of the story Grandfather Rock had shared with him. Maybe he would visit Grandfather Rock again. A blue jay landed in the tree above him and squawked at him with its braying voice.

Jak stopped and saw the blue jay twitch its head from side to side, peering at him with either eye. The bird flicked its feathers and then flew to a farther branch and brayed again. Jak grinned and started to move on, but the blue jay flew to a branch in front of him and flapped its feathers. It seemed as if the bird was trying to get his attention. Jak glanced at the blue jay, and the bird stared at him, then flew off again to the same branch it had just come from. Perhaps the blue jay wanted him to follow it. Jak moved off the path and began to make his way through the brush toward the blue jay.

After a while the blue jay flew to the top of the ravine and started to call out loudly. Jak crawled through some bushes and had to pluck off little furry burrs that stuck to his shoelaces. Trying to tie shoes with shoelaces full of burrs was very frustrating. Jak had learned that through experience. When he glanced up again, the blue jay was still gazing at him. Jak stood and trudged toward the tree the blue jay was in. When he reached the tree, he saw that the blue jay's nest was in the branches above the bird. Then he saw another blue jay looking at him over the edge of the nest. Jak realized these two blue jays were parents. One tiny head and then another peeked over the edge of the nest. Their eyes were closed and their feathers seemed moist, almost like wet fur. The blue jays parents had children! They were babies just like Joey.

Then Jak heard the all-too-familiar rumble of the big yellow machine from the other day. He sniffed the air but couldn't smell anything yet. Jak looked through the trees to the street on the other side and spotted more machines being unloaded with a lot more men in yellow hard hats waving and yelling at one another over the racket. Now the blue jays were staring at the machines, as well. Jak could practically feel their worry as the machines began to spit black smoke and position themselves facing the trees and the blue jays' home.

When Jak scanned his surroundings, he spied all sorts of animals gazing at the street above. There were squirrels, chipmunks, sparrows, and raccoons. All these animals were worried, Jak sensed. He saw it in their eyes. He felt it in the way they moved more cautiously than normal. Jak experienced their fear in his heart, but he didn't know what to do.

The machines with huge shovels positioned themselves facing the woods. It seemed to Jak that all the animals tried to make themselves smaller. Jak glanced back at the street and saw a car pull up and stop. Out of the car came Mr. Stone and Mousy Man. While Mousy Man flitted from person to person, Mr. Stone didn't move at all. Instead he seemed to stare right at Jak.

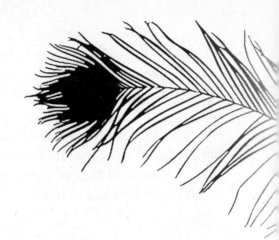

Chapter Fourteen

Jak ran as fast as he could to Grandfather Rock. When he burst into the clearing, he blurted out, "They're going to cut down all the trees! What should we do?" Only silence greeted Jak. "Grandfather Rock, did you hear me?"

"Breathe, little one," Grandfather Rock finally said. "Take your time."

"They're going to cut down all of my trees! The animals will have no homes! I won't have a place to ... to ..." Jak couldn't finish the sentence because he didn't quite know how to express what he was feeling just now.

"Who said these trees were your trees?" Grandfather Rock asked.

Jak blinked. "I don't know ... I play here. I live here. I guess I consider them my trees."

"How old are you, little one?"

"I'm twelve."

"How old are the trees?"

"I don't know."

"The trees are older than you, little one. If anything, *they* own you."

"How can they own me? I'm human. They're just ... just trees!"

"Every living thing in this place has a spirit, little one. Humans are very young compared to some of the beings in this place."

Jak glanced around and reminded himself that he was speaking to a rock. What would Christina or his parents think? At that moment Jak could have sworn Grandfather Rock laughed. Jak couldn't hear anything, but he felt a deep rumble in his chest. He even sensed it in his bones.

"Now who is going to cut down the trees?" Grandfather Rock asked.

Jak told Grandfather Rock about the earth-moving machines and the men who were driving them. "What can we do?" he asked when he finished.

"I have felt Mother Earth move differently over the past few days. Perhaps this is why."

Jak didn't have the patience to wait for Grandfather Rock to consider his words. He wanted an answer now. "I'm just a kid. I don't know how to stop the construction. I want the trees and the animals to always be here. I like the ravine the way it is."

"Just because you are small does not mean you are helpless, little one. You have a spirit, too. You are just as much a part of this place as the trees. Just ask the men to stop."

"I'm only a kid. They won't listen to me. The adults think I don't know anything yet." Again Jak experienced a deep rumbling in his chest. He was sure Grandfather Rock was chuckling! That made him more upset. Even Grandfather Rock was laughing at him!

"Little one, just because you are young, does not mean you do not know anything. Often new ideas come from the young. Sometimes adults are so consumed with their own lives that they do not take the time to listen to the young. Sometimes they are so consumed with watching over the young that they cannot see them for the new faces they are to become. There is a story of a young boy about your age who changed the lives of his people as well as the land around him. Would you like to hear it?"

Jak had a feeling Grandfather Rock was going to tell a story whether he wanted him to or not. Still, he liked the stories since they seemed to answer questions he hadn't asked yet. Actually, they seemed to answer questions he didn't even know he wanted to ask! "Are the birds going to sing again?" Jak asked. "That actually kind of freaked me out."

Again Jak heard the rumble of laughter. "I cannot say what will happen. All you should do is listen with an open heart and an open mind. Now, would you like to hear this story?"

"Yes, Grandfather Rock, I'd like to hear your story."

"So where is your gift to share with me for my story?"

Jak's heart almost stopped. He always brought something for Grandfather Rock but had forgotten to this time. "I ... I didn't bring anything. I was in too much of a hurry. I'm sorry."

"Do you believe I am older than you, little one?"

"Yes, I do."

"You must always respect your elders, for they know more about this place than you do."

Jak realized the logic of that statement. "Grandfather Rock, I'll listen with an open heart and an open mind. I won't speak. I'll just listen. Please share with me the things that you know."

Chapter Fifteen

"The Cree have been in this land for many, many turns of the seasons," Grandfather Rock began. "At the time this story took place the Cree were living on the shores of a vast lake, a body of water so wide the opposite shore could not be seen. It was harvest time, so the Cree were gathering all the food they would need for the long, cold winter nights ahead. All through the warm summer months the Cree had picked corn and wild rice and had hunted deer for meat and other gifts. The Cree had stored all this food in huts in their village, for they knew that was the key to their survival. When they collected as much as they could and the leaves had changed colours and were falling back to Mother Earth, the Cree prepared a celebration. They laughed and danced, sang and played, and did so long into the night until they were exhausted and fell into their beds.

"The Cree at this time always left a warrior to watch over their sleeping village to protect them from their enemies. That night, when the moon was high and the fires were low, a great thrashing was heard by the warrior. Tree trunks snapped and branches shattered. Then, with the help of the firelight, the warrior spied two huge red eyes peering at him out of the dark. Suddenly, more trees snapped and leaves were whipped about as if a whirlwind raged in the forest. Then out stepped a great big ... what do you think it was, little one?"

"A bear?"

"Not a bear."

"A wolf?"

"No, not a wolf. Out of the darkness stepped a giant ..."

Grandfather Rock stopped speaking, and it seemed as though the entire ravine waited on his words. Jak was about to say something when Grandfather Rock finally spoke. "Skunk!"

At these words, from behind Grandfather Rock, up jumped an actual skunk. Its little black eyes glittered in the sunlight filtering through the leaves. The skunk twitched its tail, and for some reason Jak wasn't worried. He was too busy giggling at the thought of a giant skunk coming out of the woods.

"Now this skunk was not any ordinary-sized skunk," Grandfather Rock said. "He was huge and black. And we both know what happens when a skunk lifts its tail, right?"

The skunk on Grandfather Rock's back lifted its tail, and Jak cringed, expecting to be sprayed.

"Well, this skunk was so big and so black that if you were there when he lifted his tail, you would not survive. That is how much this skunk could spray his stink."

Jak giggled again as the skunk on Grandfather Rock's back twirled in a circle.

"At that moment the young warrior let loose with a war cry and moved forward to battle the great black skunk. But all the skunk did was whip around, lift his tail, and *pffffffttt!*"

Jak giggled again.

"The young warrior fell dead," Grandfather Rock whispered.

The skunk slipped off Grandfather Rock somewhere behind and out of sight.

"The people woke the next morning to find their warrior lying in the dust surrounded by giant skunk tracks. All except one of their storage huts was empty of food, and they knew a great enemy had come to them in the night. Everyone gathered in a great council, young and old, male and female, in a great circle. They did so because in a circle there is no beginning and there is no end and everyone is equal. All were allowed to speak and share ideas. They talked and talked but could not come up with a solution to fight this giant skunk."

The skunk slipped back onto Grandfather Rock, its nose sniffing the air. Jak kept his eyes on the skunk because he still wasn't sure if he was going to be sprayed or not.

"Finally, one young boy, about your age, little one, raised his voice and said, 'I know someone who hasn't forgotten the Creator's Law of how the Elder Brother animals are here to help and guide the Younger Brothers, the people. He has quick eyes, a strong jaw, and very sharp teeth, and his name is Goongohotay, the Wolverine.'"

The skunk on Grandfather Rock immediately began to twitch its head as if looking for something ... or someone.

"The people talked and talked some more as they considered this idea. Finally, they agreed that this was their only chance to save themselves. So they sent the young boy off to find Goongohotay. The young boy ran and ran until he came to Goongohotay's den. When he got there, he called out once ..."

Something barked loudly behind Jak, and he spun around, astonished. He searched with his eyes but couldn't see anything.

"Twice ..." Grandfather Rock continued.

This time there were two barks. Jak peered deeper into the trees and bushes but still couldn't see the animal making the noise. He turned around, and the skunk on Grandfather Rock had its back hair up but its tail down. It had stopped sniffing the air and was now looking in the direction of the barking.

"Three times!" Grandfather Rock cried.

This time there were three barks, and once more Jak failed to see anything. Then the ravine got quieter and quieter, and even the trees seemed to listen to Grandfather Rock.

"Goongohotay came out of his den and stood in front of the young boy. He gazed down with questions in his eyes. The young boy glanced up and said to Goongohotay, 'I come to you on behalf of my people. There is a great black skunk that has come to our village and is eating all the food that we'll need to survive the long, cold winter nights ahead. If this continues, our people won't survive. Goongohotay, you are wise and strong. I ask you to come back to our village and help us.'"

As Grandfather Rock spoke, his voice became more hushed until he was barely whispering. Jak had to lean forward to hear his words. The ravine was totally silent now.

"Goongohotay also remembered the Creator's Law. He agreed to return to the village, and once there he gathered the people once more into a great council and said, 'I want all the very young and the very old to go off into the woods and hide. But I want the young warriors to stay on the fringes of the forest and wait for my signal. This is my signal ...'"

As Grandfather Rock finished his last words, the ravine came alive. Every bird, every squirrel, every chipmunk, every animal that could make a noise unleashed their voices. The din was so loud that Jak was surprised that the leaves stayed on the trees. Then, as soon as the noise had begun, it ceased.

"The people agreed to do as Goongohotay asked," Grandfather Rock continued. "That night the very young and the very old went off into the woods and hid. The young warriors stayed on the fringes of the forest and waited for Goongohotay's signal. Goongohotay went into the last storage hut that had food and left the door ajar so that he could see out."

All was motionless within the ravine. It seemed to Jak as though clouds had covered the sun as the ravine got darker and darker with each word Grandfather Rock uttered.

"That night, when the fires were low and the moon was high, there was a great thrashing in the woods. Trees snapped, branches broke, and out into the firelight stepped the great black ..."

"Skunk," Jak whispered.

"The great skunk lifted his nose to sniff the air and smelled the food in the one remaining storage hut. He inched closer and closer to where Goongohotay was hiding until he was only a short distance away. At that moment Goongohotay stepped out of the storage hut."

The skunk on top of Grandfather Rock stood taller.

"Goongohotay asked the skunk, 'Why have you come to the people?'"

"The skunk glared at Goongohotay, snickered, then said, 'I don't have to worry about the people! They're small and weak. They gather food for me, and that's why I'm so strong!'"

"Goongohotay knew he would have to fight the great black

skunk, but he also realized that if the skunk whipped around and lifted his tail he would not survive. So, little one, what do you think Goongohotay did?" Grandfather Rock asked.

Jak closed his eyes and thought hard. "Uh, he ran?"

"No, he did not run."

"He plugged his nose?"

"No, he did not plug his nose. Would you like to know what happened?"

Jak nodded. The skunk on Grandfather Rock shook its head, but Jak ignored him. The animal no longer worried Jak.

"Goongohotay opened his jaws as wide as they could go, so wide that the moonlight reflected off his sharp teeth. When the giant black skunk turned and lifted his tail, Goongohotay lunged forward and bit the skunk right in the butt!"

The skunk on top of Grandfather Rock immediately stuck its tail between its legs and whimpered. Jak blinked, then laughed so hard his stomach hurt. He pictured a wolverine biting the great black skunk in the middle of a Cree village. In his imagination it was hilarious!

"The skunk is not a very smart animal," Grandfather Rock said, "but he is smart enough to know it is not a good thing to have a wolverine biting your behind. That was when Goongohotay gave his signal."

The ravine around Jak burst into sound again.

"And again he gave his signal!" Grandfather Rock cried.

The ravine got louder than before, and Jak had to cover his ears this time as leaves fluttered from the trees.

"A third time!"

The skunk on Grandfather Rock had its paws over its ears. Jak had his ears covered, too. Leaves and twigs landed on the ground around them. It seemed as though it was raining, but it wasn't water. Somewhere, off in the distance, thunder rumbled over the land. Jak couldn't actually hear the thunder, but he felt it through the earth beneath his feet. He shut his eyes and began to feel fear for the first time with Grandfather Rock.

And then everything became silent once more.

Grandfather Rock continued the story. "The young warriors came out of the woods with their weapons raised to see that Goongohotay had seized the great skunk's butt with his teeth! A great battle ensued. Dust flew, trees were knocked down, and after a long and vicious battle the giant skunk lay motionless.

"The people started to laugh and dance, sing and play, and talk and eat, but what they did not see was that Goongohotay still had his jaws wrapped tightly around the great skunk. And as he loosened his grip, a little bit of skunk spray came out and hit him in the eyes, blinding him."

Jak was sad. He didn't want anything bad to happen to Goongohotay. All he did was what his heart had told him to do. Why should he be punished for that?

"The people felt very bad for Goongohotay," Grandfather Rock said. "The Cree knew he had sacrificed his eyesight so that the people could survive. They wanted to help Goongohotay, but they could not get close to him because ... well, he stank like a skunk."

Jak giggled.

"But the Cree Nation lived on a great lake that was so wide no one could see the opposite shore. The people directed Goongohotay to wash out his eyes in the clean water of the lake. For twenty-eight days and twenty-eight nights, a full cycle of Grandmother Moon, Goongohotay rinsed his eyes. When he came out of the lake, he could see again. But in washing out his eyes he had poisoned the water. He had made the water undrinkable. He had made the lake ... salty. Still, to this day, all the oceans that surround Turtle Island, or what you know as North America, are salty. Now I am done."

Jak sat still for a moment. This story had given him an idea. One boy had saved an entire village. Jak glanced around at his ravine and realized it wasn't just *his* ravine anymore. He gazed into the trees and saw the birds and squirrels. They all seemed to look back at him. Although a rock couldn't have eyes, Jak believed Grandfather Rock, too, was studying him. Even the skunk on Grandfather Rock was watching him.

"Thank you for the story, Grandfather Rock," Jak whispered.

When Grandfather Rock didn't reply, Jak slowly made his way back home. As he walked, something occurred to him. He could try to save the ravine from the construction crews! He could be just like Fox! Or the little boy in the Cree story Grandfather Rock had shared with him. Just because he was small didn't mean he didn't have a voice. He had an idea, but he had to figure out how to make it work.

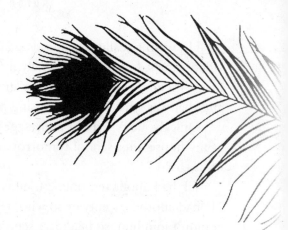

Chapter Sixteen

The basement was a dark and dank place. There were only two small windows in the entire main room. Sometimes Jak felt this room was a dungeon, but it was *his* dungeon. The basement was decorated with hockey memorabilia, since his dad was a big hockey fan and was constantly trying to get Jak to watch games with him. Posters of famous hockey players, plastic pucks, and hockey jerseys covered the walls. Even Christmas decorations of hockey players hung from the ceiling when it wasn't even Christmas!

In the middle of this miniature hockey museum stood the family's entertainment centre, with more than a hundred DVDs and video games. Jak's dad also collected movies and had hundreds of them. That was cool, Jak thought sometimes. When Jak had friends sleep over, they always had plenty of movies to watch. Jak's father had a lot of action-adventure films. Of course, the remote control always seemed to go missing. Jak was certain that remotes loved to hide from him.

He wasn't really a gamer as gamers went. Jak liked superhero video games, but he wasn't really into all of the online things most of his friends were. He did have an online email account, though, and that was what he was accessing now.

Quickly, he typed out a message to all of his friends: "Meet me at my house after school tomorrow night. I have something for all of us to do."

Jak had about ten online friends he played various games with. He had another twenty or so who were out of his area and probably couldn't join him, so he didn't send the message to them. Just then the phone rang.

"Jak, telephone for you!" his mother yelled downstairs.

"Who is it?" Jak asked.

"Come answer the phone and find out for yourself. I'm not your message service, honey."

Jak sighed and hunted for the cordless phone. The phone seemed to take pleasure in hiding from him, too. Finally, he found it and said, "Hello?"

"Hi, Jak!" Christina's voice said.

Jak froze, then said, "Uh, hello, Christina."

"So what are you doing?"

Jak was immediately suspicious. "Nothing much. Just playing a video game."

"Oh, cool! So what are you doing after school tomorrow night?"

"Uh, I'm meeting some of my friends to do something."

"Oh, yeah?" Christina said. "Like what?"

"Nothing much. I'm just going to hang around with them."

"Can I come over and hang around, too?"

Jak froze again. "Uh …"

"I won't be a problem, Jak. Is it all right if I bring along some of my friends, too?"

Suddenly, Jak realized he might be surrounded by a whole bunch of girls who would probably just talk and giggle at him. But, he thought, he had never had any real time with Christina. He always watched her from across the classroom or caught glimpses of her in the schoolyard. Jak really wanted to talk to Christina face to face. Still, it seemed to Jak that every time he thought Christina was being nice she was actually teasing him.

Jak decided to take a chance, though. "Sure, if you want to come, that's fine with me. Do you know where I live?"

"Yep, you live on the other side of the ravine. We'll be there tomorrow. See you!"

Jak stared at the phone for a moment after Christina hung up, hoping he hadn't just set himself up for a big fall.

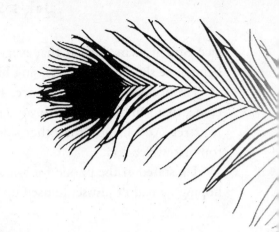

Chapter Seventeen

The next day at school Steve Burke continued to leave Jak alone. In fact, Steve didn't pay any attention to him at all. Jak didn't bother thinking about the reasons behind his enemy's change of heart. He was just happy he didn't have to worry about him today.

There were other things to fret about, starting with Christina and all her friends. She had said hello to him in the morning when she spotted him, but after that she was completely silent. That made Jak nervous. What was he thinking when he invited her over to his house? He was now certain that Christina was going to make fun of him in front of the only friends he had. Then she would tease him at school, and everyone else would think he was a geek.

But Christina wasn't what was really bothering Jak. The construction crews, Mr. Stone, and Mousy Man and what they were going to do to his ravine made him far more upset. Jak knew what he wanted to do, but he couldn't ask his parents to help because they would probably try to stop him.

While Jak mulled that over Mr. Crick came into the room and rapped his knuckles on his desk. "Class, pay attention now."

The students calmed down as much as any class of kids ever could.

"Does anyone know where the Six Nations of Grand River Territory is?" Mr. Crick asked.

Jak's classmates glanced at one another, obviously mystified.

Mr. Crick seemed disappointed, but he continued. "The Six Nations of the Grand River Territory is only twenty minutes away from here. The population of Brantford is around ninety-six thousand people. Only twenty minutes away from here more than twenty thousand First Nations people live on the Six Nations of the Grand River Territory."

The class gasped.

Mr. Crick smiled. "Surprising, isn't it? That's why we're studying the contributions of the Iroquois to Canadian history."

A hand went up, and Mr. Crick nodded. "Why are they called Six Nations when they're the Iroquois?" a student asked.

Mr. Crick smiled again. "The first European explorers to this land came from a place called France. That meant they all spoke French. They arrived first in what is now known as Quebec, which at the time was populated by the First Nations people called Ojibway or Anishinabae. They warned the French not to go south because their enemies lived there. The Anishinabae called their enemies the Iroquois, which wasn't what they called themselves. But the French continued to call them Iroquois. The British soon moved in, as well, and they came to know the Iroquois as first the Five Nations and then the Six Nations. So there were two different names for the exact same people."

As Mr. Crick said all this, he wrote the names on the chalkboard in capital letters side by side. "The Iroquois or Six Nations people had a name for themselves, too, which was Haudenosaunee. That means People of the Longhouse." Mr. Crick wrote that name beside the others.

"So the First Nations people who live only twenty minutes away from here are now known by three different names. Iroquois, a name given to them by the French. Six Nations, a name given to

73

them by the British. And Haudenosaunee, a name they've had for thousands of years.

"Most of our ancestors only came to Canada in the past two or three hundred years or even less. The country we call home, Canada, was once entirely populated by First Nations people. In fact, even the name Canada comes from First Nations people. When the Iroquois first met the French, they invited them back to their villages to speak. They called their villages *kanata*. The French thought that was the name of the land in which they had landed. The name stuck with the French, and soon this land became known as Canada."

Again the class was amazed.

"Toronto is a Native name, too. Ottawa is the name of a First Nations people who still live around our capital. Winnipeg is also a Native name. Manitoba, too, is a First Nations name. Even Ontario is a Native name! There are lots of things around us that we take for granted but which originated with First Nations people. Even Thanksgiving!"

All of the students laughed.

Mr. Crick frowned. "Don't laugh. It's true! All the foods we eat at Thanksgiving were shared with the first European explorers to this land. Turkey, wild rice, potatoes, sweet potatoes, corn, squash, and beans all originated with First Nations people. The original European explorers didn't know what to hunt, how to hunt it, or where to hunt it until First Nations people taught them. Same with farming. The European explorers didn't know what to plant, where to plant, or how to plant until First Nations people taught them. So, in reality, we wouldn't even be here if it weren't for First Nations people teaching us how to survive."

The class was listening to Mr. Crick in a way Jak had never seen before.

"The First Nations people of Canada were very respectful of the land around them. They didn't take more than they could use and they always used everything they did take so that nothing was ever wasted. They always said a prayer of thanksgiving to everything they used. So, you could say that every day for the First Nations was a day of thanksgiving."

Just then the PA system sputtered to life. "Mr. Crick?" the secretary said from the main office.

"Yes, Mrs. Watson," Mr. Crick replied.

"You have a phone call that's very important and they won't let me take a message. I'm sorry for disturbing your class."

"That's okay, Mrs. Watson. I'll be right there." Mr. Crick turned to the class. "I'll be right back. Please turn to your textbooks and begin the exercises on page 137 while I'm gone." Mr. Crick then left the room, closing the door behind him.

Jak listened as everyone around him murmured to themselves. He thought about what Mr. Crick had just said. Everything Grandfather Rock had told him was starting to make sense. Although Jak was still confused about a lot of things, he knew what he had to do.

He got out of his chair and walked to the front of the class. His fellow students were so astonished they forgot to make fun of him. Jak noticed Steve watching him, while Christina simply gazed at him in amazement.

Jak cleared his throat. "I have something I want to share that's very important to me. So please listen with open ears and open hearts. If you have any questions, I can answer them when I'm done."

The class remained quiet, and Jak told them about the ravine and the construction that was going to take place. A few of his classmates nodded in understanding. Then Jak began to tell them about the animals whose homes would be destroyed, about the trees and bushes that would be torn up, and about all the other destruction that would happen if the project took place. When Jak was finished, he remained standing at the front of the class.

"What can we do, though?" one student asked. "We're just kids. No one will listen to us."

Jak glanced from person to person. "I have an idea about what we can do, but we have to do it together. And we'll have to miss school tomorrow, which will probably get us into a lot of trouble."

A long time seemed to pass and then Steve Burke stood and walked up to Jak. For a moment Jak was worried that Steve was going to do something bad. But he merely looked at Jak, then turned to the class. "I'm not worried about getting into trouble if Jak's not."

Jak studied the faces of his classmates and saw that almost everyone was smiling.

Christine was smiling, too. "Aren't you having friends over to your house tonight?" she asked.

"Yes … yes, I am," Jak said, getting nervous once again. The girl had a knack for unsettling him.

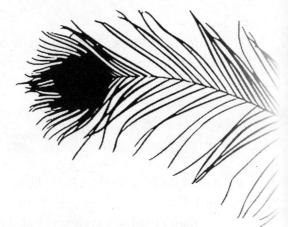

Chapter Eighteen

Jak ran into his house, dropping his backpack and lunch bag along the way. He had an excited look on his face.

When he arrived in the living room, his parents glanced at each other in puzzlement.

"Mom, Dad, I'm going to have some friends over tonight. We're going to be in the backyard, okay?"

"All right," his father said. "Who's coming over?"

"Just some friends!" Jak immediately headed for the basement. Then he halted and returned to the living room. "Uh, if it's all right, could you guys stay in the house? We kind of want to be alone."

Aaron and Barb looked at each other again, then at Jak. They nodded without saying a word. Jak grinned and raced out of the room, then came back once more to sit beside Joey. Jak's parents watched as Joey gazed up at Jak and gurgled. Jak smiled at Joey and tousled his hair. "Forgot to do that," he said. Then he got up and ran toward the basement door.

As Jak scampered down the stairs, the phone rang, and Aaron called from the living room, "Jak, phone for you!"

Jak's voice from the basement filtered up through the vents. "Thanks!"

Aaron sat beside his wife. "That was another girl on the phone for Jak."

Barb raised her eyebrows but didn't look up. She was changing Joey.

Then the phone rang again, and Aaron got up once more to answer it. "Jak, phone for you!"

"Thanks!" Jak's voice came up from the vents. "I'll answer the phone from now on, please! I'm expecting a few more calls from friends!"

Aaron returned to the couch and picked up Joey. A few minutes later the phone rang again. Aaron and Barb glanced at each other.

"What's going on?" Aaron asked as he moved toward the basement.

Barb put her hand on his arm to stop him. "Does it really matter? Jak has friends coming over. We want him to have more friends, don't we? We should just let him be."

As Joey gurgled in Aaron's arms, he nodded at his wife. Then he headed to the kitchen with his baby son to get him another bottle. Before he reached the kitchen, he passed by the living-room window that looked out onto the street and saw something surprising. Kids were riding bikes and walking toward their house. Aaron noticed a few of his neighbours out on their porches watching the parade of children. Then the phone rang once more and was immediately answered. At least twenty kids were heading to their house!

"Barb, I think you should see this," Aaron said.

His wife came over him, a quizzical expression on her face. Aaron simply motioned to the window. Barb glanced out, then moved closer to get a better look. "What do you think is going on?" she asked.

Together they watched as more and more children approached

their house. Once more the phone rang. Barb and Aaron gazed at each other, then rushed into the kitchen, opened the curtains on the window, and peered into their backyard. More than fifty children were there with bikes and skateboards. All of them were looking at Jak, who had the cordless phone in one hand and the microphone from his PlayStation 3 in the other hand. He was obviously talking to everyone, but Aaron and Barb couldn't hear a word.

"What the heck's going on?" Aaron asked, determined to get to the bottom of this.

Again Barb put her hand on her husband's arm. "Honey, please just watch. You don't have to do anything. The kids in the backyard aren't being bad. In fact, they're all listening to Jak. Have you ever seen such a thing?"

His wife was right. All the kids in the backyard were quiet as they listened to Jak. Aaron even saw Steven Burke sitting quietly. He nudged Barb and pointed at Steve. Both of them didn't really like Steve. They had heard he was a bully. So what was he doing in their backyard listening to their son?

Just then a girl with blond curls rode up on a bike with a few other girls. Jak stopped what he was doing when he noticed them. Then he grinned and motioned them to a place in front. The girls smiled at Jak and sat down. All the children were in a semicircle facing their son ... Jak.

Aaron reached out and gripped Barb's hand. Together, with Joey cradled in Aaron's other arm, they watched as Jak continued to speak. Then their son stopped talking and stared at the kids in front of him for a moment. The girl with blond curls eventually stood and walked to where Jak was. She reached out and took Jak's hand in hers. Jak seemed a little surprised.

The blond girl said something, and Jak's parents saw that all of the children were still listening. Jak nodded as the girl spoke, never taking his eyes off her. When she finished, a hush fell over everyone in the backyard.

Then Steve Burke stood and cheered. When that happened, all the other kids stood and cheered, too. Barb and Aaron were stunned. What was going on?

Just as suddenly as all the kids in the backyard had arrived, they jumped onto their bikes and skateboards and left as fast as they could. They seemed to move with one great purpose.

Aaron and Barb watched as Jak talked into the PlayStation 3 mike. When Jak was finished speaking, he looked off into the ravine. Aaron and Barb followed their son's gaze. They didn't want to budge, feeling that the slightest movement would disturb this special moment.

Then the front door banged open and Chelsey sailed into the kitchen. "What the heck's going on? I almost got run over by an army of little kids!"

Aaron and Barb glanced at their daughter, shrugged, then resumed watching Jak in the backyard as they smiled at each other.

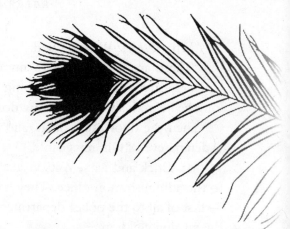

Chapter Nineteen

The next morning Mr. Crick entered the teachers' lounge before class as he usually did and made a beeline to the coffee machine to pour himself a cup. He was in a good mood the past few days because his class really seemed to be appreciating his talks about First Nations people. So, when the bell rang, Mr. Crick whistled as he headed to his class.

To his complete surprise, though, there wasn't a single student sitting at a desk when he opened the door. Mr. Crick contemplated the empty room for a moment, then glanced at his watch. Where was everybody?

Mr. Crick pushed the button on the PA system connecting his classroom to the administration office. "Mrs. Watson, there isn't an assembly or anything is there?"

"No, Mr. Crick, there isn't," Mrs. Watson told him over the PA.

Again he scanned the vacant room, then punched the PA button. "Mrs. Watson, there are no students in my classroom at the moment."

"What?" Mrs. Watson cried.

"There are no students in my classroom this morning," Mr. Crick repeated. "Is there something I should know about?" Before long he heard heavy feet running down the hall.

Then the door burst open, and Mrs. Watson stood there with widening eyes. "Oh, my gosh!"

Mr. Crick and Mrs. Watson glanced at each other and headed to the administration office. They had a lot of phone calls to make — first of all to the police department and then to all the parents of the missing children.

Mr. Stone and Mr. Shriken stepped out of their car and headed toward the construction site. All of the workers, decked out in yellow and orange hats and tool belts, were assembled there. Mr. Stone still wore his shiny sunglasses and bright yellow hard hat. He could have been made of bronze so tanned was his skin. Pablo Shriken, on the other hand, was pale and pasty and skittish. All the local residents' signatures had been received, and today was the official day for construction to begin.

A fleet of bulldozers was lined up facing the ravine, while the workers lounged casually next to their machines, waiting for Mr. Stone and Mr. Shriken to tell them to start. There wasn't a cloud in the sky. Only a slight breeze made the leaves tremble in the trees as Mr. Stone and Mr. Shriken made their way to the front of the line of machines, men, and women.

"Ladies and gentlemen, today we're going to begin creating a neighbourhood," Mr. Shriken announced. "All the necessary forms and signatures are in, and we can begin." Mr. Shriken tried to project his voice, but most of the workers had to lean forward to hear him. Many missed what he said altogether.

Mr. Stone took a step toward the machines and people. "Please be careful while you work on this site. The land is a little bit bumpy. Make sure you watch one another's backs and work together. A safe site is one where everyone works in harmony."

When the workers heard Mr. Stone's booming voice, they seemed to stand taller and listen intently. A number of men then climbed into their bulldozers and other earth-moving machines.

"Mr. Shriken, please let our people know they can start their engines," Mr. Stone said.

The little man inflated with pride. "Ladies and gentlemen, start your —" Mr. Shriken stopped in mid-sentence when he noticed no one was paying attention to him. Instead everyone was gazing beyond him at the ravine behind. He looked at Mr. Stone for reassurance, but his boss was turned toward the ravine, as well. Mr. Shriken tried to see what was causing everyone to stare. When he realized what it was, his jaw dropped.

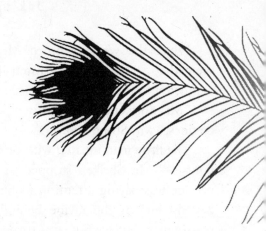

Chapter Twenty

"Now's a good time," Jak whispered. He and twenty of his friends were hidden in the trees and bushes facing Mr. Stone and Mousy Man. Jak tried to hear what Mousy Man was saying, but he couldn't understand anything. But he did hear Mr. Stone's booming voice. Then Mousy Man said a few more words, and Jak knew it was now or never.

Slowly, Jak's new friends slithered out of the trees and shuffled toward the workers and their machines. Each kid halted beside a tree or a bush. They all carried signs. Some were made of cardboard, while others were fashioned from construction paper in a rainbow of colours. At Jak's signal they all raised their signs in unison.

One sign said: TREES LIVE HERE!

Another declared: ANIMALS LIVE HERE!

A third sign announced: THIS LAND BELONGS TO RACCOONS!

The fourth sign stated: THIS TREE IS WHERE BLUE JAYS LIVE!

A fifth proclaimed: THIS LOG IS WHERE SQUIRRELS HIDE!

The sixth sign decreed: THIS TREE IS WHERE A ROBIN LIVES!

Other placards said: WHY BUILD *HERE*? or A CARDINAL LIVES HERE! or A GROUNDHOG IS UNDER YOUR FEET!

There were skater kids, rockers, boys and girls in stylish clothes, and children in just plain jeans and T-shirts. When Mousy Man finally saw what Mr. Stone and the construction workers were gaping at, he squeaked, "What the heck's going on? Who are you kids?"

Jak's father was busy working on some artwork when the telephone rang.

"Mr. Loren, it's Mrs. Watson at Woodman Drive Public School."

"Yes, Mrs. Watson, is there a problem?"

"Do you know where your son is, by any chance?"

"What do you mean? He's at school, of course."

"Mr. Loren, please don't be too upset, but Jak's entire class didn't come to school today."

"What?"

"We've informed the police, Mr. Loren. If you or your wife think of where Jak might have gone, please let them know."

Aaron disconnected immediately and called his wife at work. There was no answer, so he whipped out his cellphone and quickly texted a message: "Jak not at school. No students in his class there, either. Come home as soon as possible."

Aaron flipped the cellphone closed and got up from his desk. Joey was in a playpen in the office, and Aaron watched his younger son gurgle happily at him. *Who should he call next?* he thought frantically. Aaron didn't know what to do. Jak's entire class? How could that happen? He looked around his office and noticed that many of his artwork materials were missing: construction paper, bristol board, and even some Magic Markers and pastel crayons.

Quickly, Aaron brought Joey upstairs, dashed outside, secured his baby son in a car seat, and got behind the wheel just as his cellphone vibrated in his pocket. He flipped it open and croaked, "Hello?"

It was Barb! Police sirens echoed in the distance, and Aaron's heart somersaulted into his throat.

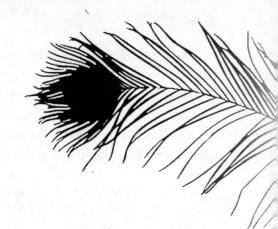

Chapter Twenty-One

Mr. Stone and Mousy Man watched as Jak approached them. On Jak's sign there was only one symbol: ?. The question mark was fluorescent pink.

At that moment a police car hurtled around the corner. Then another cruiser pulled up with a squeal of rubber on asphalt. Soon a whole lot of police officers were standing next to the workers and the bulldozers. All of the adults stared at Jak.

Finally, Mr. Stone drew closer to Jak. "Well, sonny, just what do you think you're doing?" Mr. Stone's deep voice rattled Jak for a moment.

Collecting himself, Jak looked up at the man with the shiny sunglasses. "This is where we play. This is where the animals live."

Mr. Stone crossed his arms on his chest but said nothing.

"You don't understand what happens here ... in this place," Jak said. "You just don't understand." Someone took a picture, but Jak ignored the gathering media people. "This ravine is where the animals live. The trees are older than all of us. People don't deserve this place. When you destroy this ravine, where will the animals go? You want to make new homes for people, but what about the homes already here?"

Jak glanced around. Mousy Man was gawking at him with astonishment. Then he spotted his mother. Aaron was beside her, holding Joey. Jak realized they had probably heard everything he had said. Mrs. Watson was there, too, along with Mr. Crick.

"So, kid, what exactly do you want us to do?" Mr. Stone finally asked.

More kids had arrived from all over Brantford. They carried signs, as well: I SPEAK FOR THE ANIMALS, I'M HERE BECAUSE I NEED THE ANIMALS, I'M HERE BECAUSE I NEED TREES, I'M HERE BECAUSE I GOT OUT OF SCHOOL.

Jak laughed at the last sign. Then he turned back to Mr. Stone. "If you just read all these signs with an open heart and an open mind, you'll understand what we'd like you to do."

Mr. Stone studied all the kids and their signs, but before he could say anything Mousy Man asked one of the policemen, "Officer, can you please make sure these kids get home safe? There'll be heavy machinery working through this area very shortly."

Shaking his head, Mr. Stone watched as more and more children and their parents joined the already huge crowd that had formed. He took a step back from Jak and eyed Mousy Man. "You say we have all the necessary signatures?"

"Yes, yes, absolutely, we have them all!" Mousy Man sounded a bit desperate.

Mr. Stone frowned. "I think, Mr. Shriken, that we can't have all the necessary signatures."

"What do you mean? Of course we do! We have to continue this project!"

Mr. Stone glanced down at Jak and took off his sunglasses, revealing chocolate-brown eyes. Then he pulled off his yellow hard hat under which Jak glimpsed hair as black as a raven. Finally, Mr. Stone knelt in front of Jak. "Sonny, I don't think any construction's going to happen here today."

Jak was stunned. Now that he was so close to Mr. Stone he could see that the man was First Nations! The bronzed skin wasn't a really good suntan, after all.

Mousy Man looked as if he were going to have a fit!

By this time, Aaron and Barb were standing on either side of Jak. When Mr. Stone got to his feet, he introduced himself and said, "You have a very good boy there." Then he waved one finger in a circle above his head, and all the workers took off their hard hats and moved toward their own cars. The bulldozers wouldn't be needed now.

"Wait, wait!" Mousy Man shouted. "You said we'd start working today! We can't stop now! Do you know how much money we'll lose if we stop now?"

Mr. Stone faced Mousy Man. "The kids are right, Mr. Shriken. I guess I sort of forgot about what's important. Animals need homes just like we do. We're not going to cut down any trees today. We should listen to kids more often. They can teach us a thing or two, like remembering how to look at the world around us. A world where money isn't everything. Look at all these children around us, Mr. Shriken. It makes my heart happy. It makes my spirit happy." Mr. Stone smiled at Mousy Man. "Mr. Shriken, how does *your* spirit feel after what you've seen today?"

Mousy Man was struck dumb.

Jak gazed up at his parents, and they smiled tenderly at him. All around them kids shook their signs and cheered in triumph.

At that moment Chelsey sauntered up and asked, "What the heck's going on? I was on my way to school and saw all these little kids. Is there a parade going on or something?"

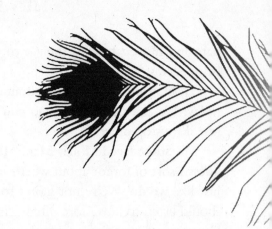

Chapter Twenty-Two

The next day was Saturday, and Jak was happier than he could ever remember being. Christina Lowman wanted to meet with him at Mohawk Park! There was still something he had to do, though. "Chelsey, can you come with me to the ravine for a while?"

His sister stared at him. "What for? I don't like mosquitoes."

"Just because, okay?"

Chelsey was curious, so she agreed, and together they picked their way through the brush in the ravine.

"Eeewww!" Chelsey cried. "There's bugs everywhere!" She took each step as though she were walking on eggshells.

"Just a little farther, Chels."

"I don't know why I'm doing this. This is disgusting. Bugs everywhere, Geez!"

"Only a little farther. Do you still have that peach I gave you?"

"Yes, I do, you little snot."

Jak smiled knowingly. "I have someone I want you to meet."

"Here? In the freaking woods? It better not be that Mr. Stone guy. He was a little scary."

Jak said nothing and took Chelsey's hand to help her clamber over a tricky log.

"Why do you spend so much time here?" Chelsey asked, wrinkling her nose. "There are disgusting things everywhere!"

Jak stopped and sat in front of a moss-covered rock.

"What are we doing here?" Chelsey asked.

"Is that a peach?" Grandfather Rock rumbled. "I haven't tasted a peach in a very long time."

Chelsey jumped back. "What was that?"

"*Awnee, sago and ske:noh,* daughter. If you share your peach with me, I will share a story with you ..."

Time of the Thunderbird
by Diane Silvey
illustrations by John Mantha
978-1-55002-792-1
$11.99

Kaya and Tala, the adventurous Coast Salish twins, are back from their exploits in *Spirit Quest* on a new mission to discover why children are disappearing from one of their tribe's villages. Earth dwarves are being blamed for the missing children, but the twins are sure they're not at fault. Something very sinister is happening, so once again the sister and brother set out with Yaket, their friend and companion, to rescue the kidnapped children. Along the way they meet a mysterious owl, a cedar ogre, demons galore, Aixos, the most ferocious of all sea serpents, and the Thunderbird himself!

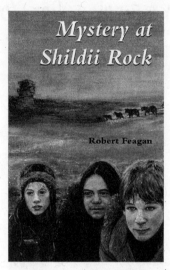

Mystery at Shildii Rock
by Robert Feagan
978-1-55002-668-9
$11.99

To the Gwich'in First Nation, Shildii Rock near Fort McPherson in the Northwest Territories is a place of deep mythological significance. When twelve-year-old Robin Harris spots someone on the rock staring at him, he just knows something is wrong. Robin and his friend Wayne Reindeer, a Gwich'in youth, set out to discover what's going on and to gain the respect of their fathers. When murder comes their way, Robin and Wayne realize it's too late to turn back. Will the boys unlock the secrets of Shildii Rock in time? Or will they, too, fall victim to a killer?